DISCARD

ll circ
01/21/09
LC

2004

DISCARD

After-School
Confidential

Also by Erik P. Kraft
Lenny and Mel
Lenny and Mel's Summer Vacation

LENNY and MEL
After-School Confidential

Story and pictures by
Erik P. Kraft

Simon & Schuster Books for Young Readers

New York London Toronto Sydney

SIMON & SCHUSTER BOOKS FOR YOUNG READERS

An imprint of Simon & Schuster Children's Publishing Division

1230 Avenue of the Americas, New York, New York 10020

SIMON & SCHUSTER BOOKS FOR YOUNG READERS is a trademark of Simon & Schuster, Inc.

Book design by Greg Stadnyk

The text for this book is set in Berkeley, Lemonade, and Flyerfonts.

The illustrations for this book are rendered in pen and ink.

Manufactured in the United States of America

10 9 8 7 6 5 4 3 2 1

Library of Congress Cataloging-in-Publication Data

Kraft, Erik P.

Lenny and Mel : after-school confidential / story and pictures by Erik P. Kraft.—1st ed.

p. cm.

Summary: Urged by their parents to join an after-school club, twin brothers Lenny and Mel are assigned by the teacher who runs the school newspaper to report on the school's other organizations.

ISBN 0-689-85109-X (hardcover)

[1. Clubs—Fiction. 2. Schools—Fiction. 3. Journalism—Fiction. 4. Brothers—Fiction. 5. Twins—Fiction.] I. Title.

PZ7.K85843 Lf 2004

[Fic]—dc22

2003013571

To Collin

CONTENTS

NOT AGAIN!

Ah, summer vacation. A time to sit back and do nothing. A time to avoid schoolyard bullies and homework. A time that always ends too soon.

"Who's excited to go back to school?" asked Lenny and Mel's father.

"Is that a trick question?" asked Lenny.

"Not really," said their father.

"Not me," said Mel.

"Well, your mother and I were thinking . . ." their father started to say.

Uh-oh, thought Lenny. *They're up to something.*

". . . that you guys might like school a little bit more if you were to join a club."

"Aw, man," said Lenny.

"Come on, it'll be fun," said their father. "You'll meet new people and learn new skills."

"Is there a monkey club?" asked Mel.

"I don't think so," said their father.

"That's the club I want to join," said Mel.

"Where are you going to get monkeys?" asked Lenny.

"We don't really need monkeys," said Mel. "We can just sit around and draw monkeys and talk about monkeys. And maybe write letters to monkeys—if anyone knows one."

"You need to join a club that the school offers," said their father. "You can talk to one of the teachers if you need help choosing one. We'll pick you up at the school once you get out."

"There better be a monkey club," said Mel.

"Oh, it's you two," said the principal, Mr. Fudgerson.

"Our parents said we have to join an after-school club," said Lenny.

"We need help choosing one," said Mel.

"Well, detention is always very popular," said Mr. Fudgerson. "But hopefully you wouldn't be there every day. Anyway, the

school newspaper usually writes about the clubs. If I had a paper, you could look in there." He thought for a minute. "Or you could just go join the school newspaper. They're a club. They probably need people. Do you like to write about stuff?"

"We can do that," said Lenny.

"So, why don't you give it a shot?" asked Mr. Fudgerson.

"This just in—okay!" said Mel.

"He said school newspaper, not TV news," said Lenny.

"Thank you, Lenny," said Mel. "Now, let's see what's on in the world of sports."

"Let's go," said Lenny.

NEWSIES

The boys walked into the newspaper office. Mr. Fudgerson hadn't mentioned that Ms. Handsaw ran the newspaper.

"What do you two want?" said Ms. Handsaw. "Detention is down the hall."

"We need to waste time after school," said Lenny.

"Mr. Fudgerson said that this is the place," said Mel.

"Hmmph," said Ms. Handsaw. "Well, I don't want you two just hanging around here bothering me. You have to do work." She looked at a list on her desk. "Here, someone

needs to interview the new gym teacher. Take this notebook and go."

Lenny picked up the notebook, and they headed off to the gym.

"Are you Mr. Nizbecki?" Mel said to the sweaty man sitting on the gym floor.

"Yes, I am," said the man.

"Have you been exercising?" asked Lenny.

"No," said Mr. Nizbecki. "The heater in my office is broken. I can't turn it off."

"Oh," said Lenny.

"You have a big hole in your sweatpants," said Mel.

"Yes," said Mr. Nizbecki. "My neighbor's dog decided he wanted to eat my pants. I wasn't able to get away fast enough."

"Why did he want to eat your pants?" asked Lenny. "Did you have a hamburger in your pocket?"

"Sweatpants don't have pockets," said Mr. Nizbecki. "Well, at least not the kind I like. Anyway, what can I do for you boys?"

"We're here to interview you for the school paper," said Mel.

"Oh," said Mr. Nizbecki. "Well, what would you like to know?"

The boys thought for a minute. They hadn't planned this far ahead.

"Um, do you like teaching gym?" asked Lenny.

"Yes," said Mr. Nizbecki.

"Have you been teaching for a long time?" asked Mel.

"Yes, I have," said Mr. Nizbecki.

The boys thought for a little while longer.

"Have you ever eaten a whole pie?" asked Mel.

"A big pie or a little pie?" asked Mr. Nizbecki.

"Any pie will do," said Mel.

"Hmm," said Mr. Nizbecki. "I suppose I have."

There was a long silence.

"I guess that's it," said Lenny. "Thank you for your time."

The boys went back to the newspaper room.

"There's still time left," said Ms. Handsaw. "Work on your story until it's time to go."

The boys sat down with their notebook and wrote away.

Exciting New Gym Teacher
By Lenny and Mel

Mr. Nizbecki is the new gym teacher. He has been teaching gym for a while, but not long enough that he is able to outrun dogs. In his spare time he eats whole pies and sews the holes in his sweatpants. Hooray for Mr. Nizbecki, even if he sweats too much.

THAT'S DEBATABLE

"Sewing sweatpants? Pies?" said Ms. Handsaw, reading the boys' article. "I think you guys might be cut out for other things than teacher interviews."

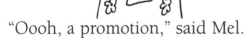

"Oooh, a promotion," said Mel.

"Yeah, sure," said Ms. Handsaw. "Anyway, it's the newspaper's job to write stories about the different school clubs and what they do. I understand you're here because Mr. Fudgerson couldn't find a paper with any of these club listings. So, I thought you boys might like to get out of my sight for a while and find out what the clubs are all about. Take your time—and if you like one, feel free to stay there."

"Ooh, investigative journalism," said Mel.

"Like on TV," said Lenny.

"Chess Team," said Mel. "Fun time or deadly sport?"

"Don't get carried away," said Ms. Handsaw. "Stick to the facts."

"Facts," said Mel. "Are they true . . . or are they deadly?"

"Okay, anyway," said Ms. Handsaw, "Debate Club meets down the hall. Why don't you start there? I think you'll find it's not very deadly at all."

"That's not going to sell many papers," said Lenny.

"The school paper is free," said Ms. Handsaw. "We don't need to get readers by running scary stories. Now, get reporting."

Lenny and Mel walked down the hall. "Hey, we can't let them know we're from the paper," said Lenny. "If we're really going to be investigative reporters, we need to be sneaky. That way we'll get the real deal. Follow my lead."

The boys walked into the Debate Club room. "We're joining this club," said Lenny, winking at Mel.

"Wonderful," said the teacher. "My name is Mr. Hen. For now you can sit and listen to the other debates and see how it's done."

They sat down and listened.

Two students were debating whether or not school uniforms were a good idea. Mel wondered if they meant superhero uniforms, and he decided it was a good thing. That way students could fly from class to class. Then he spent the rest of the time imagining himself flying in circles around the cafeteria while the other students were trying to hit him with doughnuts.

Lenny paid at least enough attention to notice that the people took turns saying they were right and the other person was wrong. Then he got distracted by wondering if the school uniforms involved cowboy hats and those glasses that have the fake noses and mustaches. He thought they would look good, but they might be kind of hot in warm weather. No one likes a sweaty nose.

"Lenny and Mel," said Mr. Hen. "How would you like to give it a try? Pick a subject that interests you, and one of you argue for it and one against it."

"Okay," said Lenny. He and Mel whispered briefly, then walked up to the two podiums at the front of the room.

"The case for Mel to clean his room," said Lenny. "Mel's room is a big mess. He should clean it. I went in there the other day to look for a book. Under a pile of clothes I found something that I think was once a taco. It was not a taco anymore. If this keeps up, he will get squirrels in there. Or worse, coyotes. This is a safety hazard. Therefore, he should clean. Thank you."

Mr. Hen looked confused. "Mel, do you have a rebuttal?"

"Yes. This is untrue," said Mel. "I do not have tacos in my room. No tacos means no coyotes. Therefore, I should be allowed to keep my room messy. And anyway, coyotes are very interesting. I think we could learn a lot by watching them eat in my room. Thank you."

Mr. Hen looked even more confused. "Um, would you like to respond, Lenny?"

"No," said Lenny. "I agree with him that coyotes are very interesting."

"Er, okay then," said Mr. Hen. "Take your seats."

Debate Club

By Lenny and Mel

Debate Club is a lot of people hanging around talking. Today they talked about school uniforms and if they are a good idea. They probably are, if the cape is the right size. If it isn't, you will probably look silly. Be sure to try on your cape before wearing it to school. Also, Mel should clean his room.

GLEE!

Lenny and Mel walked into the auditorium. There were about five people sitting around.

"Is this the Glee Club?" asked Lenny.

"Yes," said one girl. "The teacher will be here soon if you want to join."

"Hmm, time for some unsupervised questions," Lenny whispered to Mel.

"Good idea," Mel whispered back.

"Okay," Lenny said to the girl. "What exactly is *glee*?"

"I don't know," she said.

"Glee," said Mel. "What you don't know could kill you."

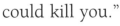

"What's he talking about?" the girl asked.

"Don't mind him," said Lenny. "So, what do you do in this club if you don't know what glee is?"

"We sing songs," said the girl.

"Glee," said Mel. "Singing? Or something more sinister?"

"Nope, just singing," said the girl.

"Knock it off," said Lenny. "You're scaring people."

"If all you do is sing, why don't they call it the Singing Club?" asked Mel.

"I don't know," said the girl. "I guess Glee Club is easier to print on the T-shirts."

"I see," said Lenny. "Thank you for your candid answers."

Glee Club

By Lenny and Mel

These people do not know what they're talking about. If you don't know what you're talking about, Glee Club is for you. That's all we can tell you.

BUT IS IT ART?

"What club will you be reporting on today, boys?" asked Ms. Handsaw.

"Is there a Sit-and-Do-Nothing Club?" asked Mel.

"Let's just save ourselves some time and assume you've already tried that one," said Ms. Handsaw. "Why don't you go see Mrs. Fujimoto in the art room? It's not really a club, but she lets students who need to hang around after school work on art projects. Like if they can't get a ride home until late. Some people don't know they can do this."

"Hmmm, secret art class, eh?" said Mel.

"It's not supposed to be a secret," said

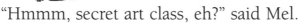

Ms. Handsaw. "That's why we need you to write an article about it."

"Interesting," said Lenny.

The boys walked into the art room. "We're here to . . . uh, wait for our parents to come pick us up," said Mel in his best I-am-not-an-investigative-journalist voice. "We would like to have something to do until they show up."

"Okay," said Mrs. Fujimoto. "Why don't we try some soap carving?"

"What are we supposed to make?" asked Lenny.

"Anything you want," said Mrs. Fujimoto.

"Anything?" asked Mel.

"Sure. Do whatever you want."

The boys looked at the bars of soap in front of them and then began whittling away furiously.

A little while later Mrs. Fujimoto came back over. "How is the soap going?"

"I think we're done," said Lenny.

She looked at Mel's soap. He had cut the bar into a bunch of tiny rectangles. "What did you make, Mel?"

"I cut the big soap into a lot of smaller soaps. For people who have trouble with, or are afraid of, big soaps."

Tiny, unthreatening soaps

"That would be very helpful for the soap-challenged," said Mrs. Fujimoto. "That was very thoughtful of you. What did you make, Lenny?"

"I made a bunch of things that look like food," said Lenny, "in case you are going to get your mouth washed out with soap. This makes it seem more like you're eating." He pointed at some of his carvings. "That's a banana, that's a hot dog, and that's a bone. It was supposed to be a chicken leg, but I got a little carried away."

Banana

Hot dog

OOPS

"Okay, boys, you did very well today," said Mrs. Fujimoto. "Come back if you need something to do after school again."

The boys' father pulled up in front of the school to get them. "What club did you guys go to today?"

"It wasn't really a club," said Lenny.

"It was Once-in-a-While-After-School Art," said Mel.

"I didn't know they offered that," said their father.

"Few do," said Mel. "This is where we come in. We're journalists." He and Lenny gave each other a thumbs-up. "Anyway, I made you some small soaps."

"Ooh, nice and little just the way I like," said their father.

After-School Art

By Lenny and Mel

Can't decide on a club to join? Too
lazy to show up to regular meetings?
Missed the bus? Have we got a club
for you. Well, it's not a club. So, I
guess we don't have a club for you.
But we can tell you about a place
where you can go once in a while
after school if you need to. You can
go and do art stuff in Mrs. Fujimoto's
room. You heard it here first.

NOW YOU'RE COOKING

Lenny and Mel stood looking at the giant pancake in their giant pan.

"I don't think we were supposed to dump all of the batter in at once," said Lenny.

"Shhh," said Mel. "I think I'm onto something."

"What's going on here?" said Mrs. Mayer, the Home Economics teacher. She eyed the giant pancake. "You were supposed to make a dozen pancakes."

"Behold!" shouted Mel. "The pancake pizza!"

"Excuse me?" said Mrs. Mayer.

"Instead of wasting your time with lots of little pancakes, why not just give everyone a slice of a big one?" said Mel.

Lenny was impressed. Mrs. Mayer, not so much. "Well, you get a few points for originality, but you were supposed to follow the assignment," she said.

"Some people don't know a good thing when they see it," said Mel.

Cooking Club

By Lenny and Mel

Someday man will invent a giant pancake log from which you will be able to slice off as many pancakes as you want. Until then you can learn to make the little ones yourself in the Cooking Club.

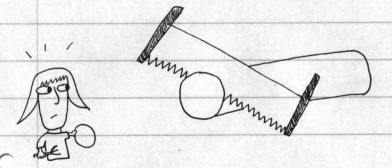

POETRY CLUB FREAK-OUT!

"Hey there, kiddos," said the teacher as the boys walked into the room.

"Hello," said Lenny.

"Is this the Poetry Club?" asked Mel.

"Sure is," said the teacher. "I'm Mr. D'Addio."

"We would like to join this club," said Lenny.

"Far out," said Mr. D'Addio.

"Where is everyone?" asked Mel.

"No one seems to stick around," said Mr. D'Addio. "I don't dig."

"There's digging involved in this club?"

asked Lenny, getting ready to make for the door.

"No," said Mr. D'Addio. "I meant I don't understand. Hey, let's write some poetry."

"That's what we're here for," said Mel.

Mr. D'Addio handed them some paper. "Go nuts," he said.

"Mel already has," said Lenny, giggling.

"Shh," said Mel. "I'm creating."

Mr. D'Addio scribbled away on his own piece of paper too.

"Hey, let's have a reading," said Mr. D'Addio when everyone looked done. He pointed at Lenny. "You go first."

"I did a haiku," said Lenny, "because I excel at them. Okay, here I go.

"What is with this club?
Where are all the other kids?
Must be seeking glee."

"Oh yeah, the Glee Club," said Mr.
D'Addio. "Right on." He pointed to Mel.
"Your turn."

Mel cleared his throat.

> *"I'm afraid of bugs.*
> *And I'm afraid of bees.*
> *And I'm afraid of dogs.*
> *The kind that can climb trees.*

"It's not totally finished
yet," Mel said.

"Is it time to go now?"
asked Lenny.

"I still have to read my poem," said Mr.
D'Addio.

"Oh," said Lenny.

Mr. D'Addio suddenly jumped up on a desk.

"Why do I scare people so much?
Blammo!
Nobody home!
Be bop a wham a doo!
Club cancelled! Free time for me!
Skippity doo blatt!
Time to go!"

Lenny and Mel were staring at Mr. D'Addio with their mouths wide open.

"You're not coming back, are you?" Mr. D'Addio said.

"Sorry," said Lenny.

"You're a little intense," said Mel.

Poetry Club

By Lenny and Mel

The faint of heart

Wazoo wazoo

Join other clubs

Pow!

We mean it!

Stand on desks! Yell!

Scare other kids!

What a club!

FARMS OF THE FUTURE

"Farmers?" said Mel, looking at the list of clubs. "I've never seen a farm in here. Where are they going to hide a farm in school?"

"Well, that's what we're here to find out," said Lenny. He knocked on the classroom door.

"Are you here to farm?" said a boy, opening the door.

"Uh, sure," said Lenny.

"Well, come on in," said the boy. "I'm Gilbert. I'm the president of the Future Farmers." The boys walked into the room.

"Are the other members late?" asked Mel.

"Um, there are no other members," said Gilbert.

"Is that how you got the president job?" asked Lenny.

"Yes," said Gilbert.

"Nice," said Mel.

"So, where is the farm?" asked Lenny.

"Right over here," said Gilbert. He led them over by the window. There was a cage with two guinea pigs in it and a couple of plants next to that.

"You farm guinea pigs?" said Mel.

"Yes," said Gilbert. "The school doesn't have room for real pigs."

"What does the bacon taste like?" asked Lenny, shuddering.

"I bet the ham is sandwich-size," said Mel.

"I don't eat them," said Gilbert. "I just take care of them."

"Phew," said the boys.

"What do you feed them?" asked Lenny.

"Just guinea-pig food and some carrots," said Gilbert. "Someday I hope to be able to grow my own carrots, but until then I have to rely on donations from my parents, or other sources."

"You mean like the salad bar in the cafeteria?" said Mel.

"Shhh!" said Gilbert. "Don't tell anyone. Food isn't supposed to leave the lunchroom."

Lenny looked at one of the plants next to the guinea-pig cage. "Hey, this plant is plastic," he said.

"Yeah, I don't have to worry about the plastic plants dying," said Gilbert. "They're easier to take care of."

"So, are there any new projects in store for the Future Farmers?" asked Mel.

"Well, I hope to be able to save enough money to buy some heavy cream," said Gilbert. "Then I could make butter. I've been saving my empty soda cans. Then I'll turn them in for the deposit and use that money."

HEAVY CREAM FUND

"Wouldn't it just be easier to not buy a soda or two and then use that money?" said Mel.

"Wow," said Gilbert. "You should be in the Accountants Club."

Future Farmers

By Lenny and Mel

They may be the Future Farmers Club, but they don't seem to be doing much farming in the present. Come on down, but when you do, bring a carrot. Guinea pigs don't like to eat plastic plants.

DINNER

"So, how's the school paper going?" asked their mother.

"Good," said Lenny.

"Are you still working on the club stories?" asked their father.

"Yes," said Lenny. "There are an awful lot of clubs."

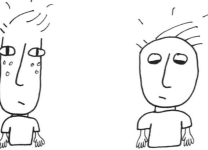

"I think there are too many," said Mel. "I don't know if we'll ever finish. What if we don't, and they make us stay in school forever?"

"I don't think that will happen," said their mother. "You haven't eaten very much," she said, looking down at his plate. "Don't you like it?"

"Tonight's dinner," said Mel. "By Mel. Tonight's dinner is good. I am worried about the club stories. Will we ever finish them? If I worry so much, will I not finish my dinner? Also, I would like some pudding."

"Mel," said Lenny. "By Lenny. Mel is losing it."

"Knock it off, you two," said their father. "You're supposed to be having fun with this. It's just a club. They're not going to hold you back over it. You can join another club if this one is making you worry too much."

"We've already joined a bunch of clubs and quit them," said Lenny. "I hope we don't have a reputation."

"Well, if they don't tell you what the clubs are, you should be allowed to try them first," said their mother. "Worrying is silly. Now, let me go see if I've got some pudding."

YOU'RE DREAMING, MEL

Mel was tossing and turning. "Too many clubs," he mumbled to himself.

"Tiny bathing suit," said a spooky voice.

"Who said that?" Mel asked.

"Nobody," said the voice.

Mel turned around. Lenny was crouched down, holding a microphone. "Uh-oh," Lenny said.

"What's going on?" said Mel.

"You joined the Swim Team, but our school doesn't have a pool," said Lenny.

"Well, I guess that's okay, as long as we don't mind losing a lot," said Mel.

"Also, as I was pointing out, there is the issue of the tiny bathing suit," said Lenny.

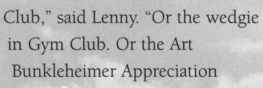

Mel looked down, then screamed.

"It's better than Dance Club," said Lenny. "Or the wedgie in Gym Club. Or the Art Bunkleheimer Appreciation Society."

"So many clubs," said Mel.

"There are more than we'd thought," shouted Lenny from far away.

50

Mel looked up. Lenny was on top of a big tower.

"What are you doing up there?" Mel yelled.

"This is the book of clubs," said Lenny. "I'm starting at the beginning. It's also the first book to read for the Book Club."

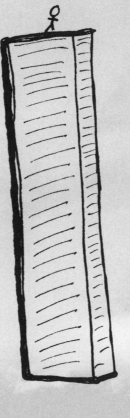

Mel climbed up the side of the book. "You can see our house from here," he said.

He got to the top. "You should join the Diving Team," said Lenny. "They also wear tiny bathing suits." Then he pushed Mel.

"Try it!"

Luckily Mel landed in a pile of dirty clothes in his bedroom.

"I'm trying to eat in here!" said a voice. A coyote climbed out of the pile. "Sheesh."

"Sorry," said Mel.

"It's time to get up," said the coyote.

"What?" said Mel.

"I said it's time to get up," said their father. "Why are you looking at me like that?"

It's time to get UP!

CLUB CLUB

"Well, boys," said Ms. Handsaw, "I have good news and bad news."

"We'll take the good news," said Mel.

"Leave the bad news for the Bad News Club," said Lenny.

"Well, the good news and bad news are sort of the same thing," said Ms. Handsaw.

"News," said Mel. "Good . . . or bad?"

"Anyway," said Ms. Handsaw, "you did a good job, but there are only the two of you, and there are a lot of clubs. It would take all year to cover them all. Mr. Fudgerson has decided to have a club fair instead of running the stories every so often in the paper. The teachers were starting to get tired of people joining their clubs for a day or two and then quitting. At least the teachers who run the clubs that you covered."

Lenny and Mel nodded.

"Then what are we going to write about now?" asked Lenny.

"Clubs," said Mel. "What the Club Fair doesn't want you to know."

"Ah, yes," said Lenny. "What this school needs is a Club Watchdog Club." And they walked down to Mr. Fudgerson's office to see about setting one up.